My Little Pony: Friendship is Magic Vol. 13

WRITTEN BY **Heather Nuhfer**

ART BY **Brenda Hickey**

COLORS BY **Heather Breckel**

LETTERS BY **Neil Uyetake**

EDITED BY **Bobby Curnow**

 Spotlight

ABDOBOOKS.COM

Reinforced library bound edition published in 2019 by Spotlight, a division of ABDO, PO Box 398166, Minneapolis, Minnesota 55439. Spotlight produces high-quality reinforced library bound editions for schools and libraries.
Published by agreement with IDW.

Printed in the United States of America, North Mankato, Minnesota.
092018
012019

THIS BOOK CONTAINS
RECYCLED MATERIALS

Licensed By:

Library of Congress Control Number: 2018940477

Publisher's Cataloging-in-Publication Data

Names: Cook, Katie, author. Nuhfer, Heather, author. | Price, Andy; Breckel, Heather; Uyetake, Neil; Hickey, Brenda; Mebberson, Amy, illustrators.
Title: My little pony: friendship is magic / writers: Katie Cook; Heather Nuhfer; art: Andy Price; Heather Breckel; Neil Uyetake; Brenda Hickey; Amy Mebberson.
Description: Minneapolis, MN : Spotlight, 2019 | Series: My little pony: friendship is magic set 2
Summary: Welcome to Ponyville, home of Twilight Sparkle, Rainbow Dash, Rarity, Fluttershy, Pinkie Pie, Applejack, and all your other favorite ponies! When evil forces threaten the ponies' good life, it's up to the Mane Six to use the Magic of Friendship to face new challenges and conquer their fears.
Identifiers: ISBN 9781532142253 (v. 9; lib. bdg.) | ISBN 9781532142260 (v. 10; lib. bdg.) | ISBN 9781532142277 (v. 11; lib. bdg.) | ISBN 9781532142284 (v. 12; lib. bdg.) | ISBN 9781532142291 (v. 13; lib. bdg.) | ISBN 9781532142307 (v. 14; lib. bdg.) | ISBN 9781532142314 (v. 15; lib. bdg.) | ISBN 9781532142321 (v. 16; lib. bdg.)
Subjects: LCSH: My Little Pony (Trademark)--Juvenile fiction. | Hardware stores--Juvenile fiction. | Ponies--Juvenile fiction. | Fireworks--Juvenile fiction. | Dating--Juvenile fiction. | Love--Juvenile fiction. | Kings, queens, rulers, etc.--Juvenile fiction | Pirates--Juvenile fiction. | Book-worms--Juvenile fiction. | Libraries--Juvenile fiction. | Comic books, strips, etc.--Juvenile fiction.
Classification: DDC 741.5--dc23

Spotlight

A Division of ABDO
abdobooks.com

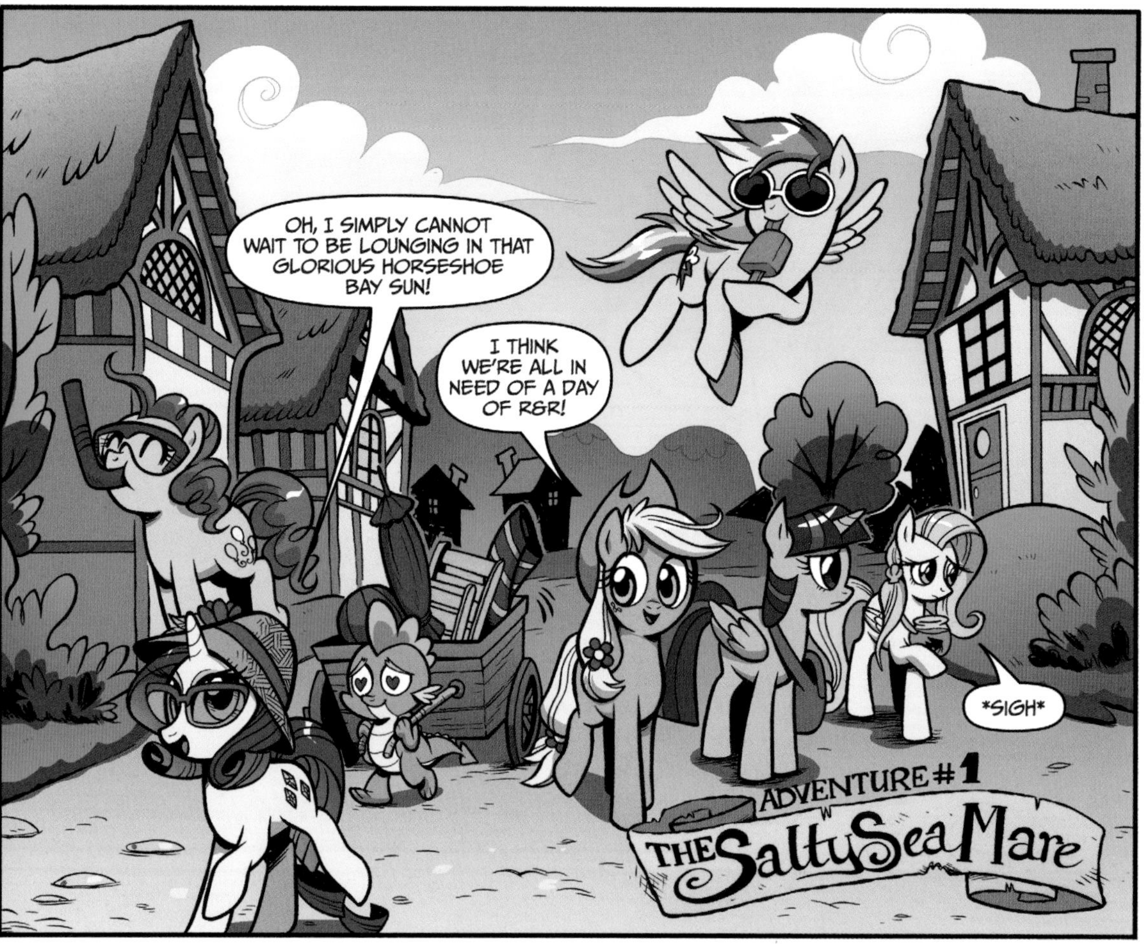
OH, I SIMPLY CANNOT WAIT TO BE LOUNGING IN THAT GLORIOUS HORSESHOE BAY SUN!
I THINK WE'RE ALL IN NEED OF A DAY OF R&R!
SIGH
ADVENTURE #1
THE Salty Sea Mare

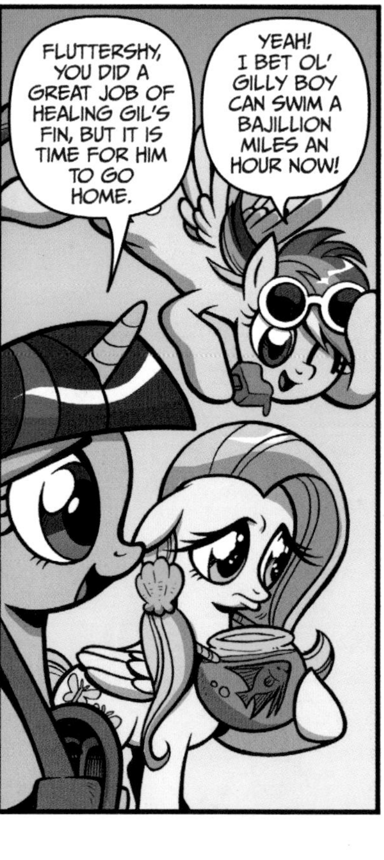
FLUTTERSHY, YOU DID A GREAT JOB OF HEALING GIL'S FIN, BUT IT IS TIME FOR HIM TO GO HOME.
YEAH! I BET OL' GILLY BOY CAN SWIM A BAJILLION MILES AN HOUR NOW!

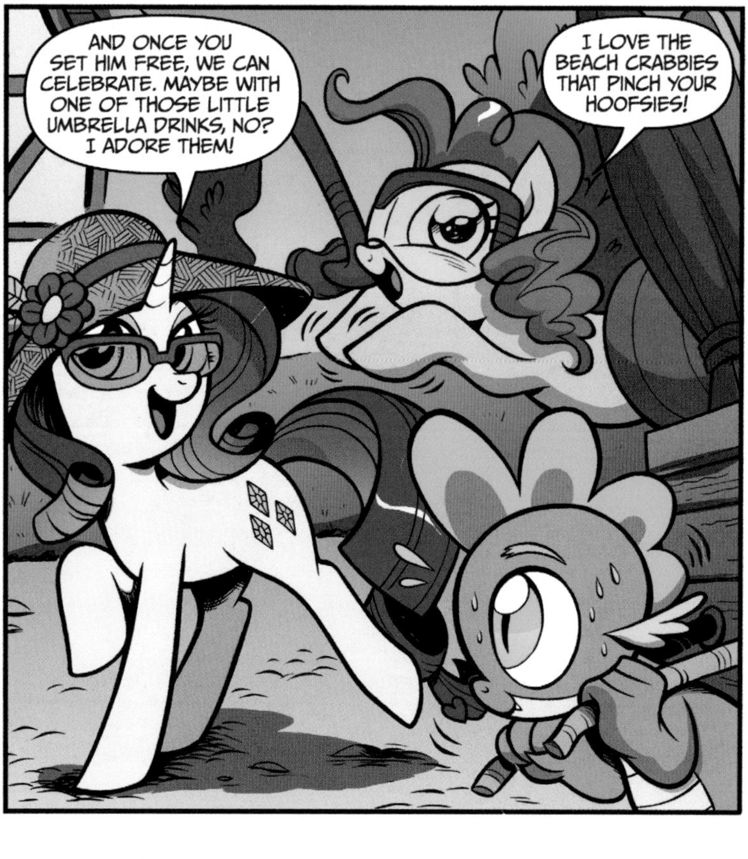
AND ONCE YOU SET HIM FREE, WE CAN CELEBRATE. MAYBE WITH ONE OF THOSE LITTLE UMBRELLA DRINKS, NO? I ADORE THEM!
I LOVE THE BEACH CRABBIES THAT PINCH YOUR HOOFSIES!

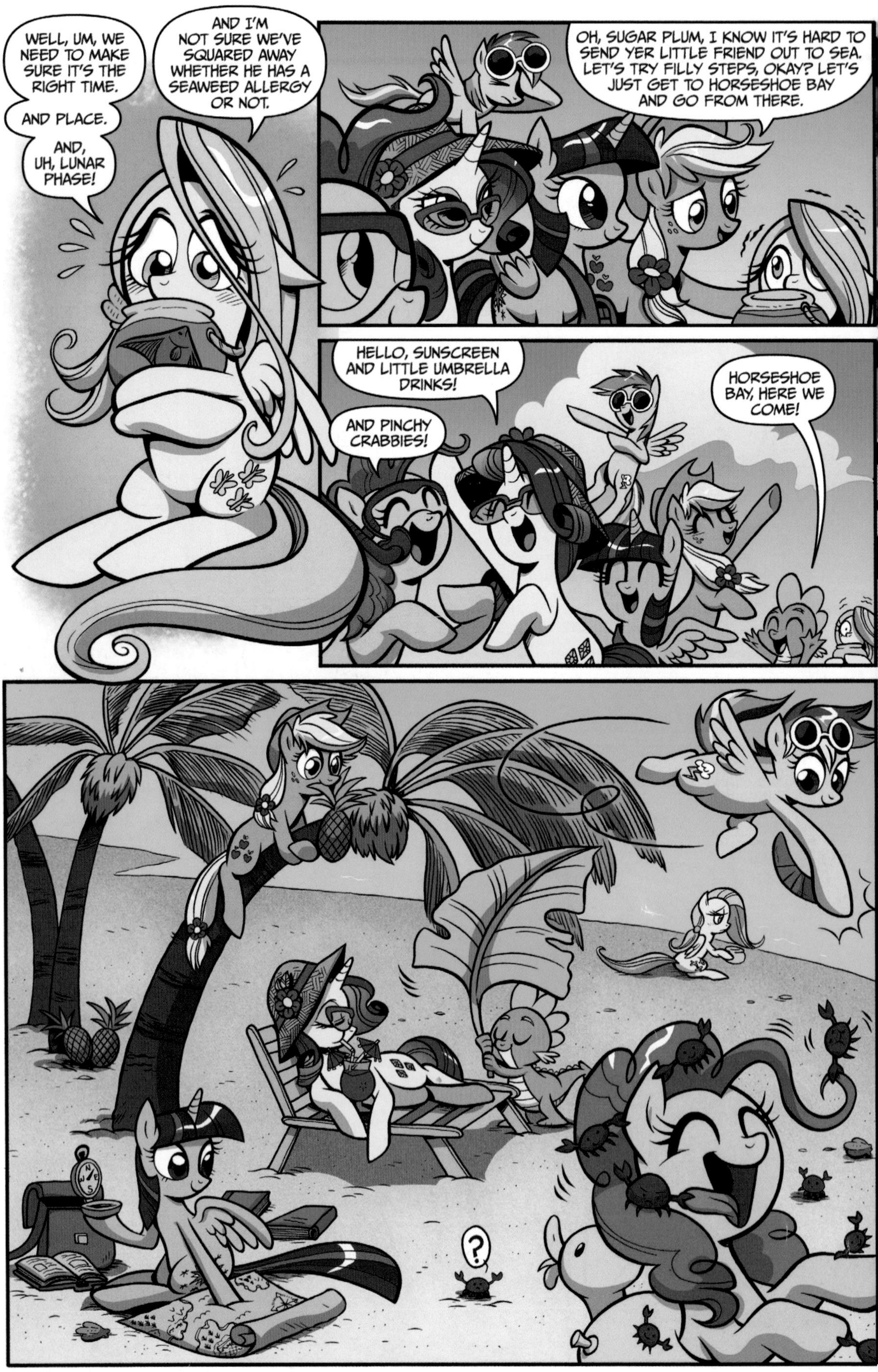
WELL, UM, WE NEED TO MAKE SURE IT'S THE RIGHT TIME.
AND PLACE.
AND, UH, LUNAR PHASE!
AND I'M NOT SURE WE'VE SQUARED AWAY WHETHER HE HAS A SEAWEED ALLERGY OR NOT.
OH, SUGAR PLUM, I KNOW IT'S HARD TO SEND YER LITTLE FRIEND OUT TO SEA. LET'S TRY FILLY STEPS, OKAY? LET'S JUST GET TO HORSESHOE BAY AND GO FROM THERE.
HELLO, SUNSCREEN AND LITTLE UMBRELLA DRINKS!
AND PINCHY CRABBIES!
HORSESHOE BAY, HERE WE COME!
?

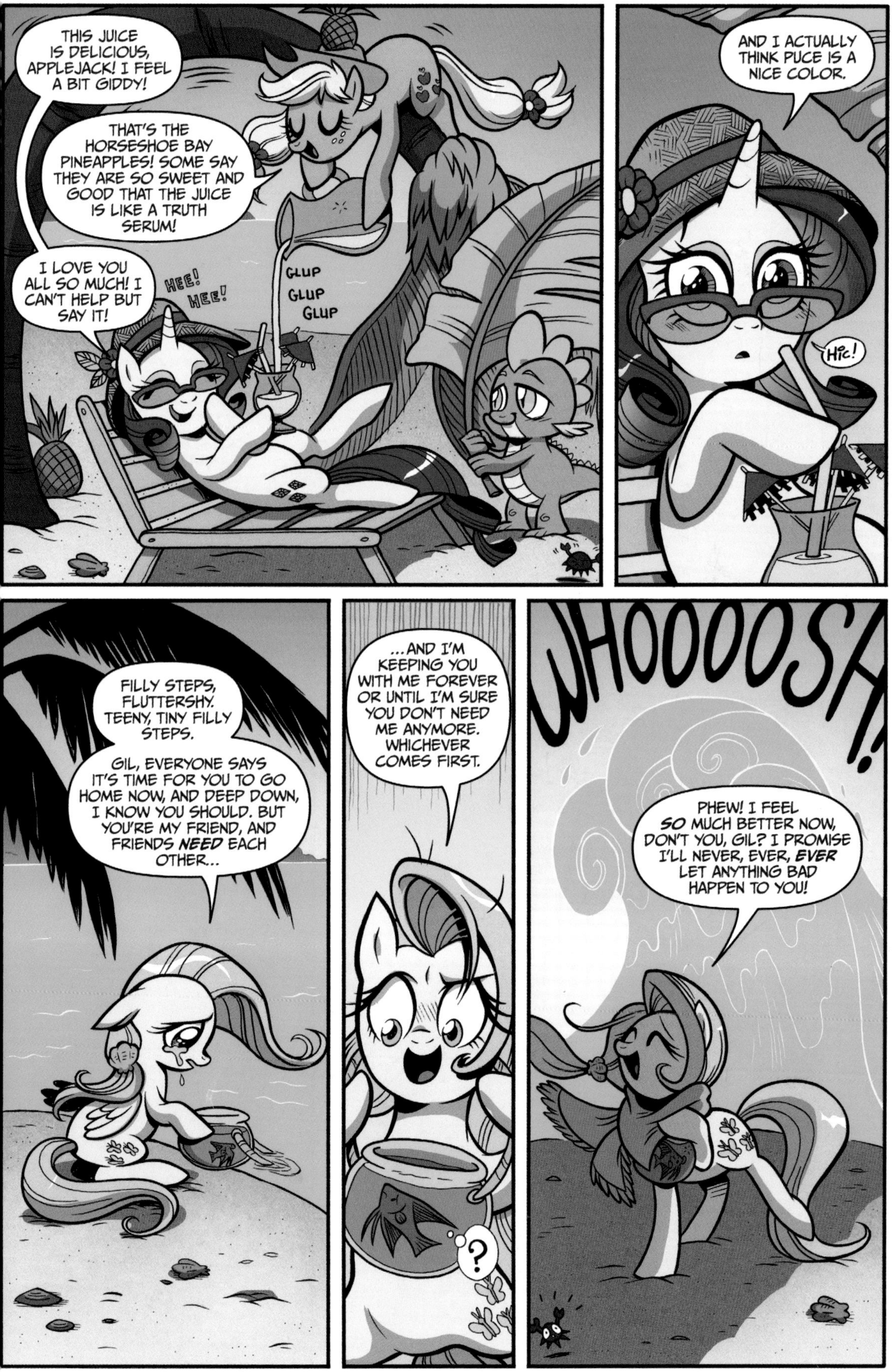
THIS JUICE IS DELICIOUS, APPLEJACK! I FEEL A BIT GIDDY!
THAT'S THE HORSESHOE BAY PINEAPPLES! SOME SAY THEY ARE SO SWEET AND GOOD THAT THE JUICE IS LIKE A TRUTH SERUM!
I LOVE YOU ALL SO MUCH! I CAN'T HELP BUT SAY IT!
HEE! HEE!
GLUP GLUP GLUP
AND I ACTUALLY THINK PUCE IS A NICE COLOR.
Hic!
FILLY STEPS, FLUTTERSHY. TEENY, TINY FILLY STEPS.
GIL, EVERYONE SAYS IT'S TIME FOR YOU TO GO HOME NOW, AND DEEP DOWN, I KNOW YOU SHOULD. BUT YOU'RE MY FRIEND, AND FRIENDS NEED EACH OTHER...
...AND I'M KEEPING YOU WITH ME FOREVER OR UNTIL I'M SURE YOU DON'T NEED ME ANYMORE. WHICHEVER COMES FIRST.
?
WHOOOOSH!
PHEW! I FEEL SO MUCH BETTER NOW, DON'T YOU, GIL? I PROMISE I'LL NEVER, EVER, EVER LET ANYTHING BAD HAPPEN TO YOU!

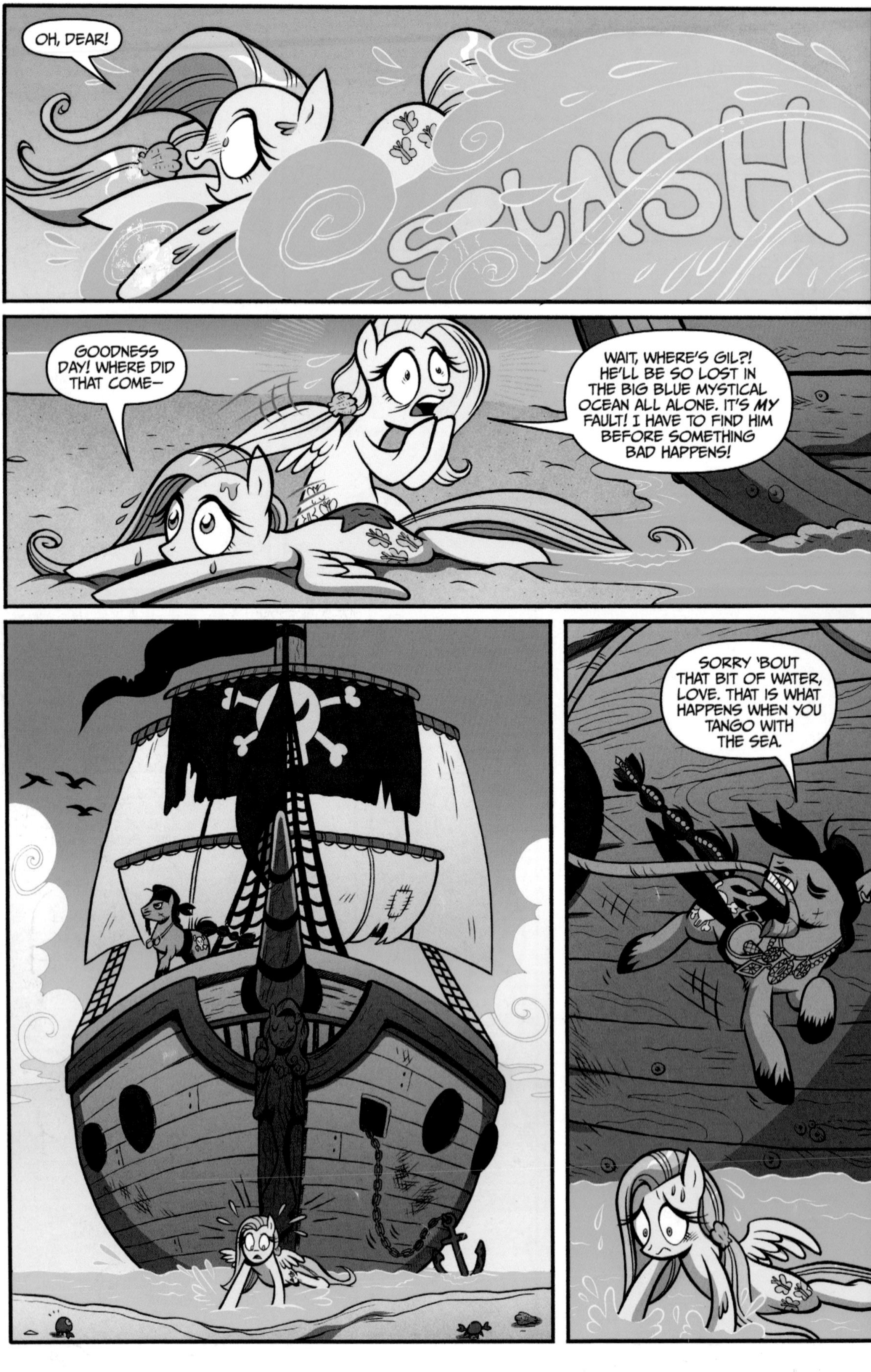
OH, DEAR!
SPLASH
GOODNESS DAY! WHERE DID THAT COME–
WAIT, WHERE'S GIL?! HE'LL BE SO LOST IN THE BIG BLUE MYSTICAL OCEAN ALL ALONE. IT'S *MY* FAULT! I HAVE TO FIND HIM BEFORE SOMETHING BAD HAPPENS!
SORRY 'BOUT THAT BIT OF WATER, LOVE. THAT IS WHAT HAPPENS WHEN YOU TANGO WITH THE SEA.

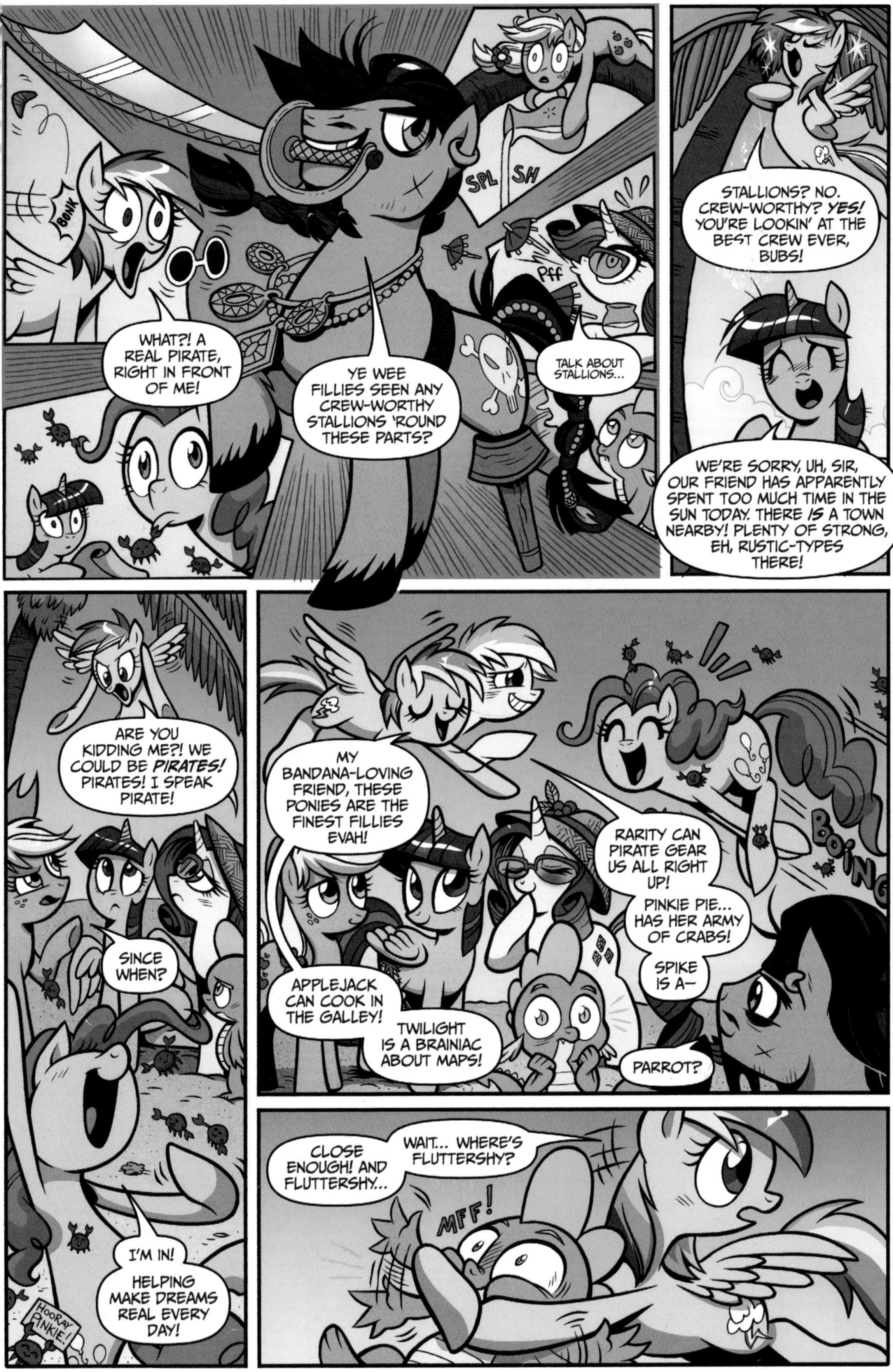
BONK
SPLSH
Pff
WHAT?! A REAL PIRATE, RIGHT IN FRONT OF ME!
YE WEE FILLIES SEEN ANY CREW-WORTHY STALLIONS 'ROUND THESE PARTS?
TALK ABOUT STALLIONS...
STALLIONS? NO. CREW-WORTHY? *YES!* YOU'RE LOOKIN' AT THE BEST CREW EVER, BUBS!
WE'RE SORRY, UH, SIR, OUR FRIEND HAS APPARENTLY SPENT TOO MUCH TIME IN THE SUN TODAY. THERE *IS* A TOWN NEARBY! PLENTY OF STRONG, EH, RUSTIC-TYPES THERE!
ARE YOU KIDDING ME?! WE COULD BE *PIRATES!* PIRATES! I SPEAK PIRATE!
SINCE WHEN?
I'M IN!
HELPING MAKE DREAMS REAL EVERY DAY!
HOORAY PINKIE!
MY BANDANA-LOVING FRIEND, THESE PONIES ARE THE FINEST FILLIES EVAH!
APPLEJACK CAN COOK IN THE GALLEY!
TWILIGHT IS A BRAINIAC ABOUT MAPS!
RARITY CAN PIRATE GEAR US ALL RIGHT UP!
PINKIE PIE... HAS HER ARMY OF CRABS!
SPIKE IS A—
BOING
PARROT?
CLOSE ENOUGH! AND FLUTTERSHY...
WAIT... WHERE'S FLUTTERSHY?
MFF!

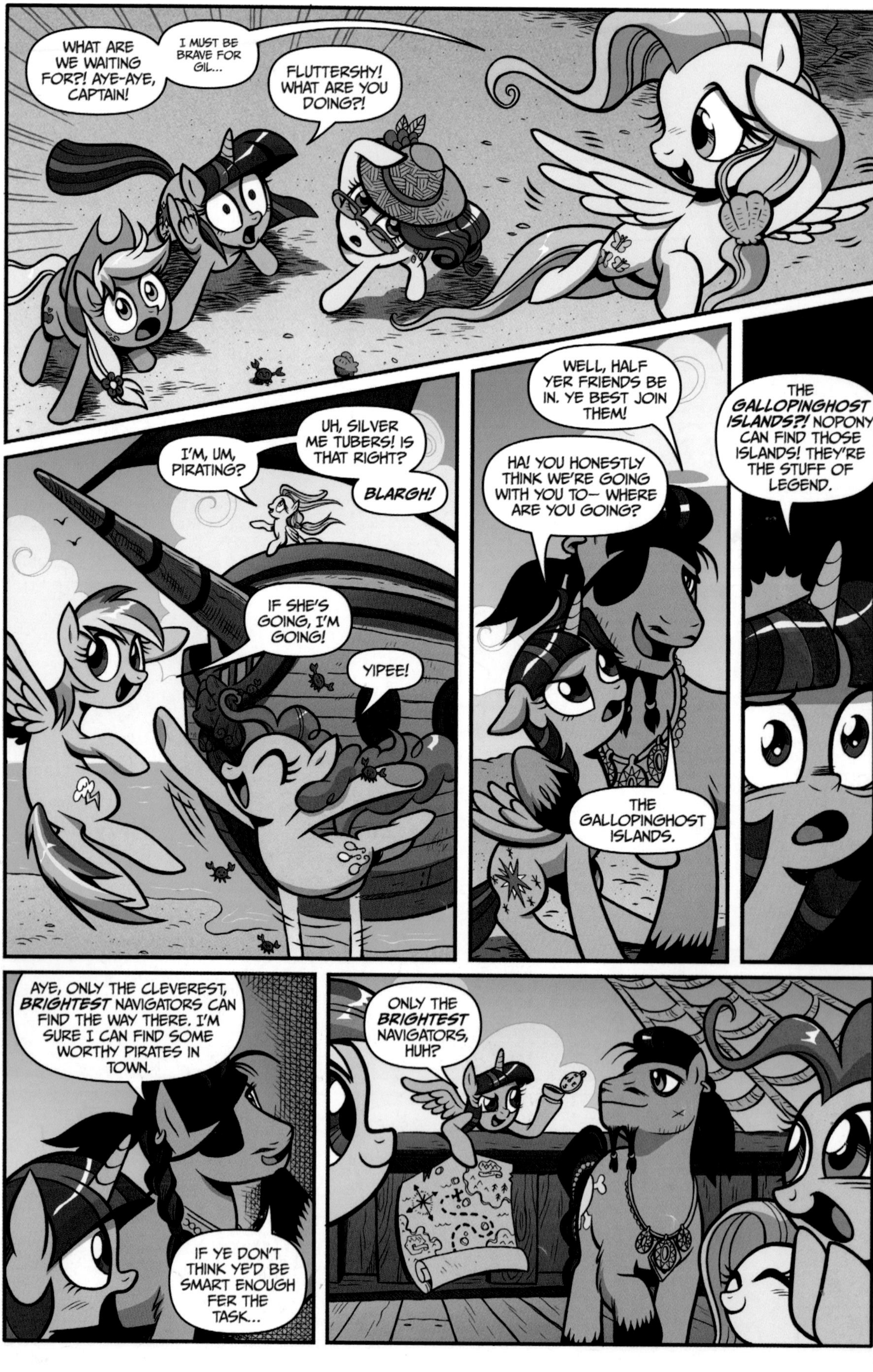
WHAT ARE WE WAITING FOR?! AYE-AYE, CAPTAIN!
I MUST BE BRAVE FOR GIL...
FLUTTERSHY! WHAT ARE YOU DOING?!
I'M, UM, PIRATING?
UH, SILVER ME TUBERS! IS THAT RIGHT?
BLARGH!
IF SHE'S GOING, I'M GOING!
YIPEE!
WELL, HALF YER FRIENDS BE IN. YE BEST JOIN THEM!
HA! YOU HONESTLY THINK WE'RE GOING WITH YOU TO— WHERE ARE YOU GOING?
THE GALLOPINGHOST ISLANDS.
THE GALLOPINGHOST ISLANDS?! NOPONY CAN FIND THOSE ISLANDS! THEY'RE THE STUFF OF LEGEND.
AYE, ONLY THE CLEVEREST, BRIGHTEST NAVIGATORS CAN FIND THE WAY THERE. I'M SURE I CAN FIND SOME WORTHY PIRATES IN TOWN.
IF YE DON'T THINK YE'D BE SMART ENOUGH FER THE TASK...
ONLY THE BRIGHTEST NAVIGATORS, HUH?

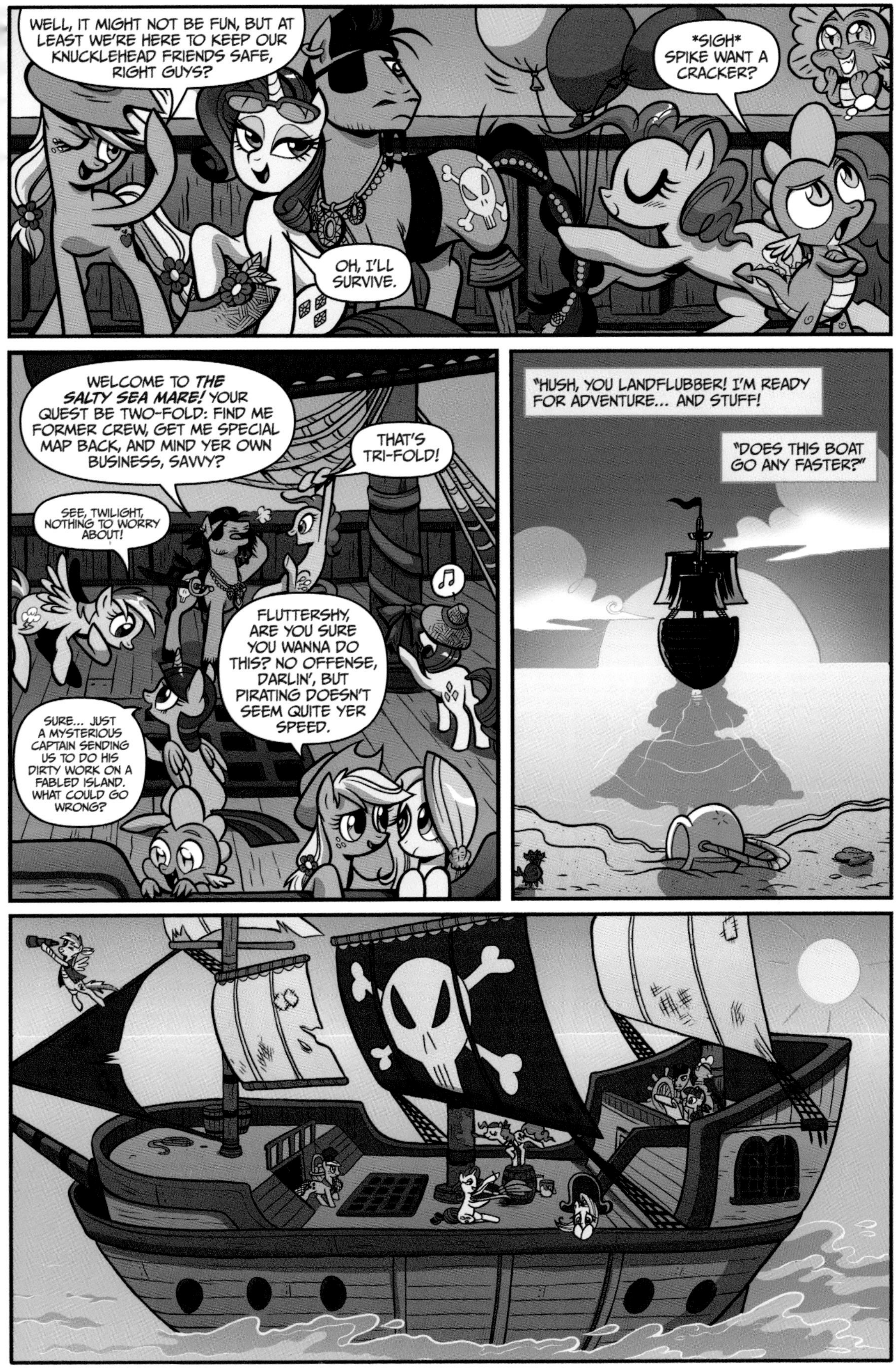

WELL, IT MIGHT NOT BE FUN, BUT AT LEAST WE'RE HERE TO KEEP OUR KNUCKLEHEAD FRIENDS SAFE, RIGHT GUYS?
OH, I'LL SURVIVE.
SIGH SPIKE WANT A CRACKER?
WELCOME TO *THE SALTY SEA MARE!* YOUR QUEST BE TWO-FOLD: FIND ME FORMER CREW, GET ME SPECIAL MAP BACK, AND MIND YER OWN BUSINESS, SAVVY?
THAT'S TRI-FOLD!
SEE, TWILIGHT, NOTHING TO WORRY ABOUT!
FLUTTERSHY, ARE YOU SURE YOU WANNA DO THIS? NO OFFENSE, DARLIN', BUT PIRATING DOESN'T SEEM QUITE YER SPEED.
SURE... JUST A MYSTERIOUS CAPTAIN SENDING US TO DO HIS DIRTY WORK ON A FABLED ISLAND. WHAT COULD GO WRONG?
"HUSH, YOU LANDFLUBBER! I'M READY FOR ADVENTURE... AND STUFF!
"DOES THIS BOAT GO ANY FASTER?"

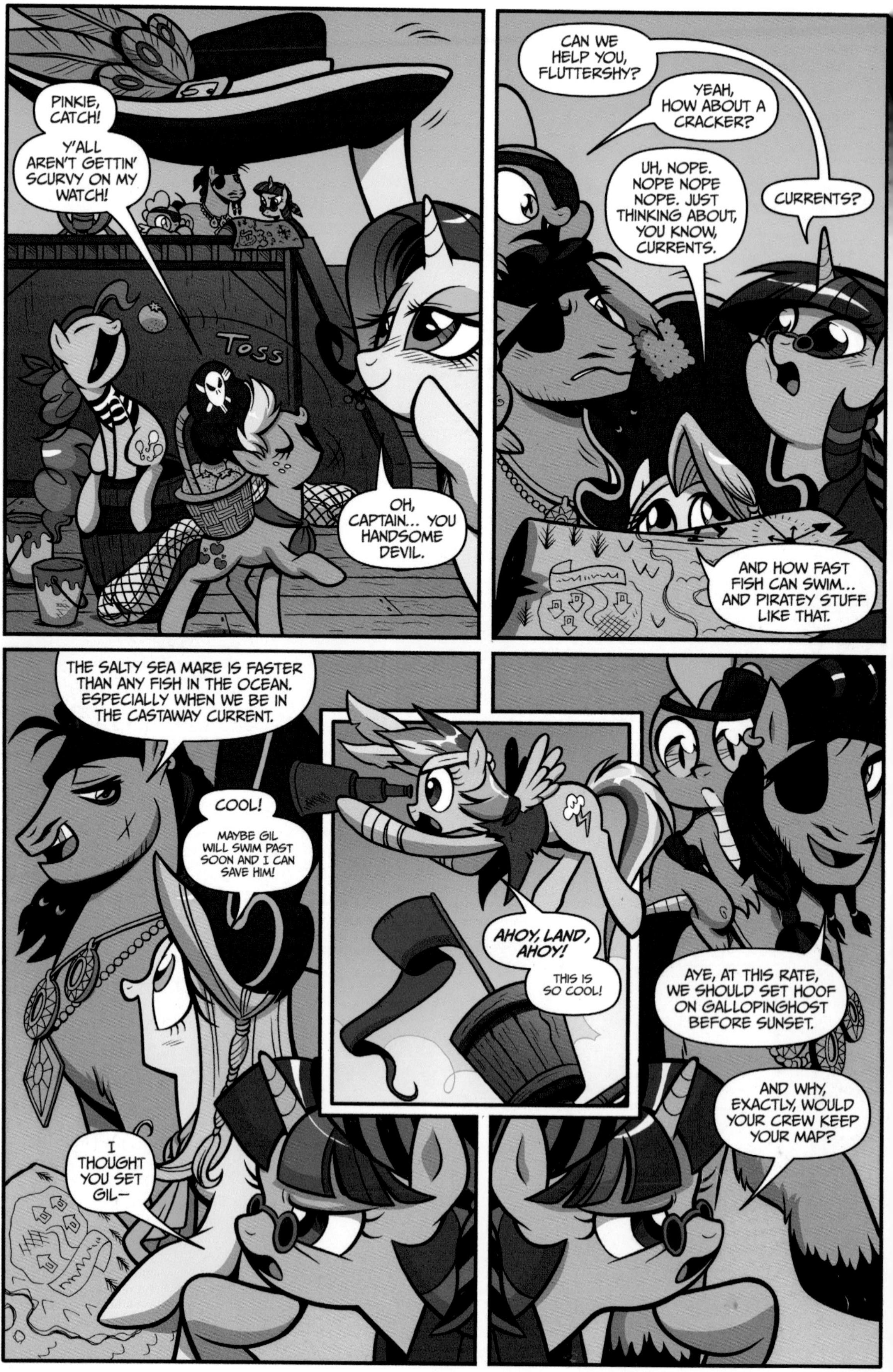
PINKIE, CATCH!
Y'ALL AREN'T GETTIN' SCURVY ON MY WATCH!
TOSS
OH, CAPTAIN... YOU HANDSOME DEVIL.
CAN WE HELP YOU, FLUTTERSHY?
YEAH, HOW ABOUT A CRACKER?
UH, NOPE. NOPE NOPE NOPE. JUST THINKING ABOUT, YOU KNOW, CURRENTS.
CURRENTS?
AND HOW FAST FISH CAN SWIM... AND PIRATEY STUFF LIKE THAT.
THE SALTY SEA MARE IS FASTER THAN ANY FISH IN THE OCEAN. ESPECIALLY WHEN WE BE IN THE CASTAWAY CURRENT.
COOL!
MAYBE GIL WILL SWIM PAST SOON AND I CAN SAVE HIM!
AHOY, LAND, AHOY!
THIS IS SO COOL!
AYE, AT THIS RATE, WE SHOULD SET HOOF ON GALLOPINGHOST BEFORE SUNSET.
I THOUGHT YOU SET GIL—
AND WHY, EXACTLY, WOULD YOUR CREW KEEP YOUR MAP?

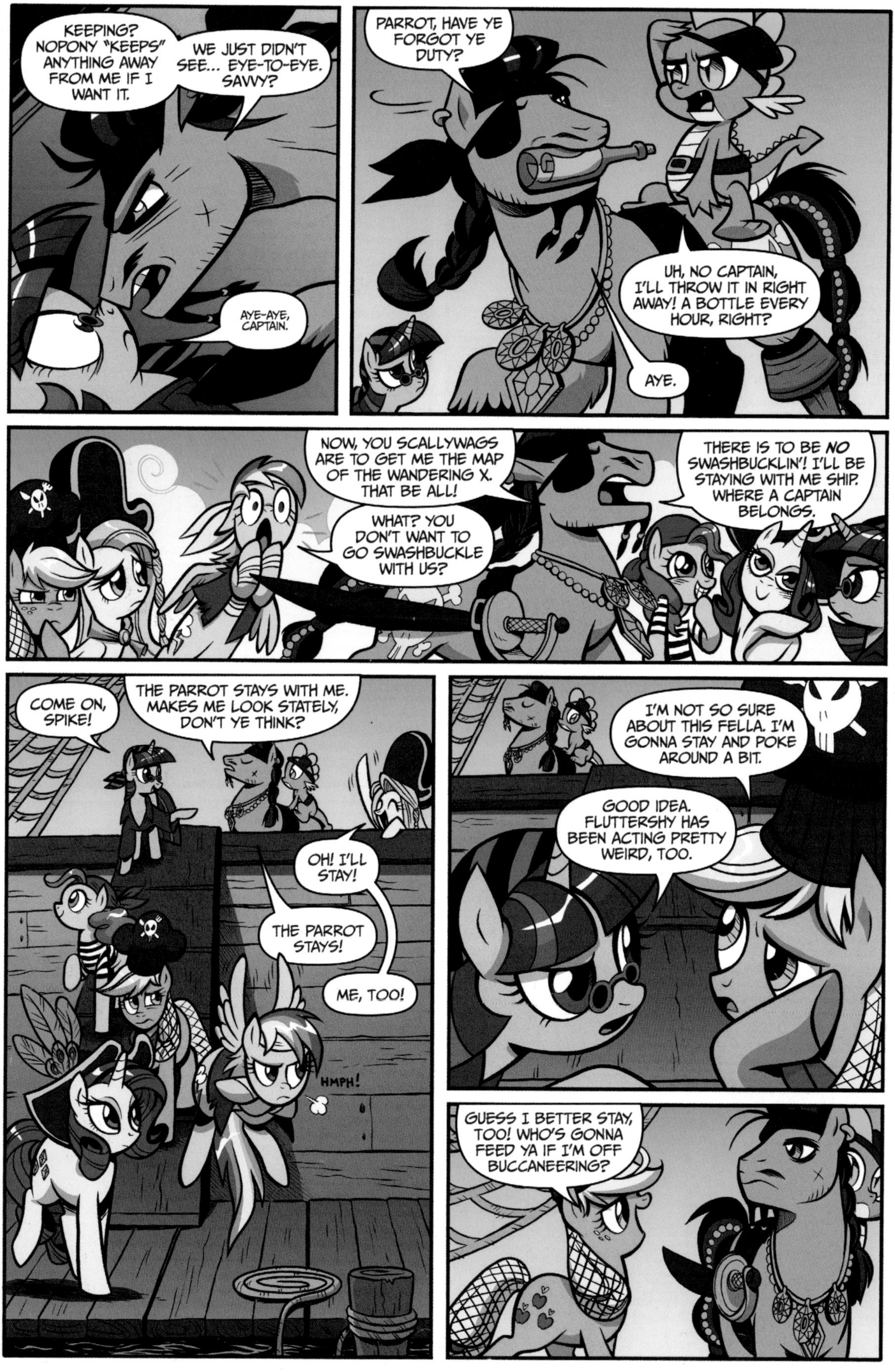
KEEPING? NOPONY "KEEPS" ANYTHING AWAY FROM ME IF I WANT IT.
WE JUST DIDN'T SEE... EYE-TO-EYE. SAVVY?
AYE-AYE, CAPTAIN.
PARROT, HAVE YE FORGOT YE DUTY?
UH, NO CAPTAIN, I'LL THROW IT IN RIGHT AWAY! A BOTTLE EVERY HOUR, RIGHT?
AYE.
NOW, YOU SCALLYWAGS ARE TO GET ME THE MAP OF THE WANDERING X. THAT BE ALL!
THERE IS TO BE NO SWASHBUCKLIN'! I'LL BE STAYING WITH ME SHIP. WHERE A CAPTAIN BELONGS.
WHAT? YOU DON'T WANT TO GO SWASHBUCKLE WITH US?
COME ON, SPIKE!
THE PARROT STAYS WITH ME. MAKES ME LOOK STATELY, DON'T YE THINK?
OH! I'LL STAY!
THE PARROT STAYS!
ME, TOO!
HMPH!
I'M NOT SO SURE ABOUT THIS FELLA. I'M GONNA STAY AND POKE AROUND A BIT.
GOOD IDEA. FLUTTERSHY HAS BEEN ACTING PRETTY WEIRD, TOO.
GUESS I BETTER STAY, TOO! WHO'S GONNA FEED YA IF I'M OFF BUCCANEERING?

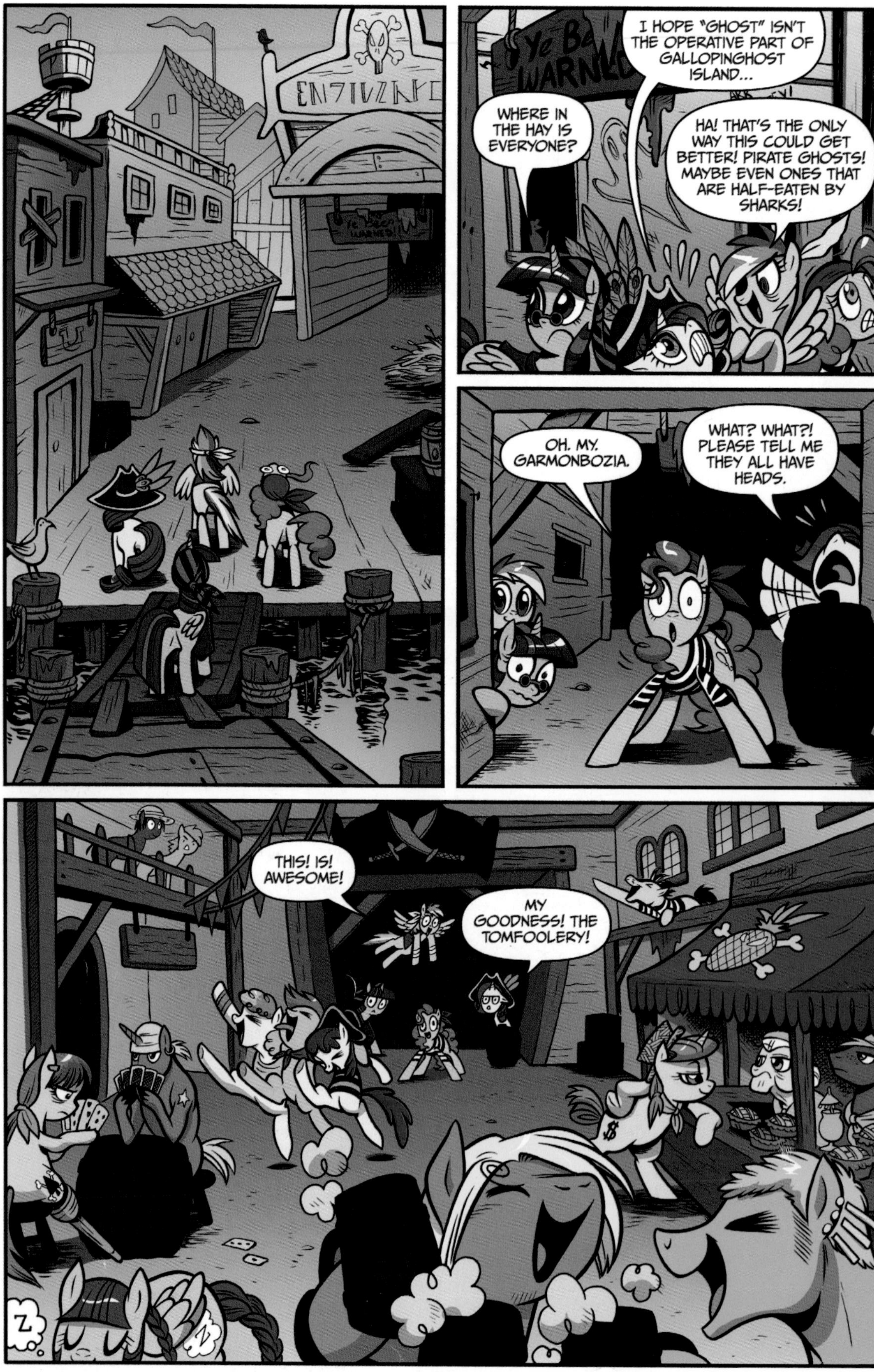
WHERE IN THE HAY IS EVERYONE?
I HOPE "GHOST" ISN'T THE OPERATIVE PART OF GALLOPINGHOST ISLAND...
HA! THAT'S THE ONLY WAY THIS COULD GET BETTER! PIRATE GHOSTS! MAYBE EVEN ONES THAT ARE HALF-EATEN BY SHARKS!
OH. MY. GARMONBOZIA.
WHAT? WHAT?! PLEASE TELL ME THEY ALL HAVE HEADS.
THIS! IS! AWESOME!
MY GOODNESS! THE TOMFOOLERY!
Z

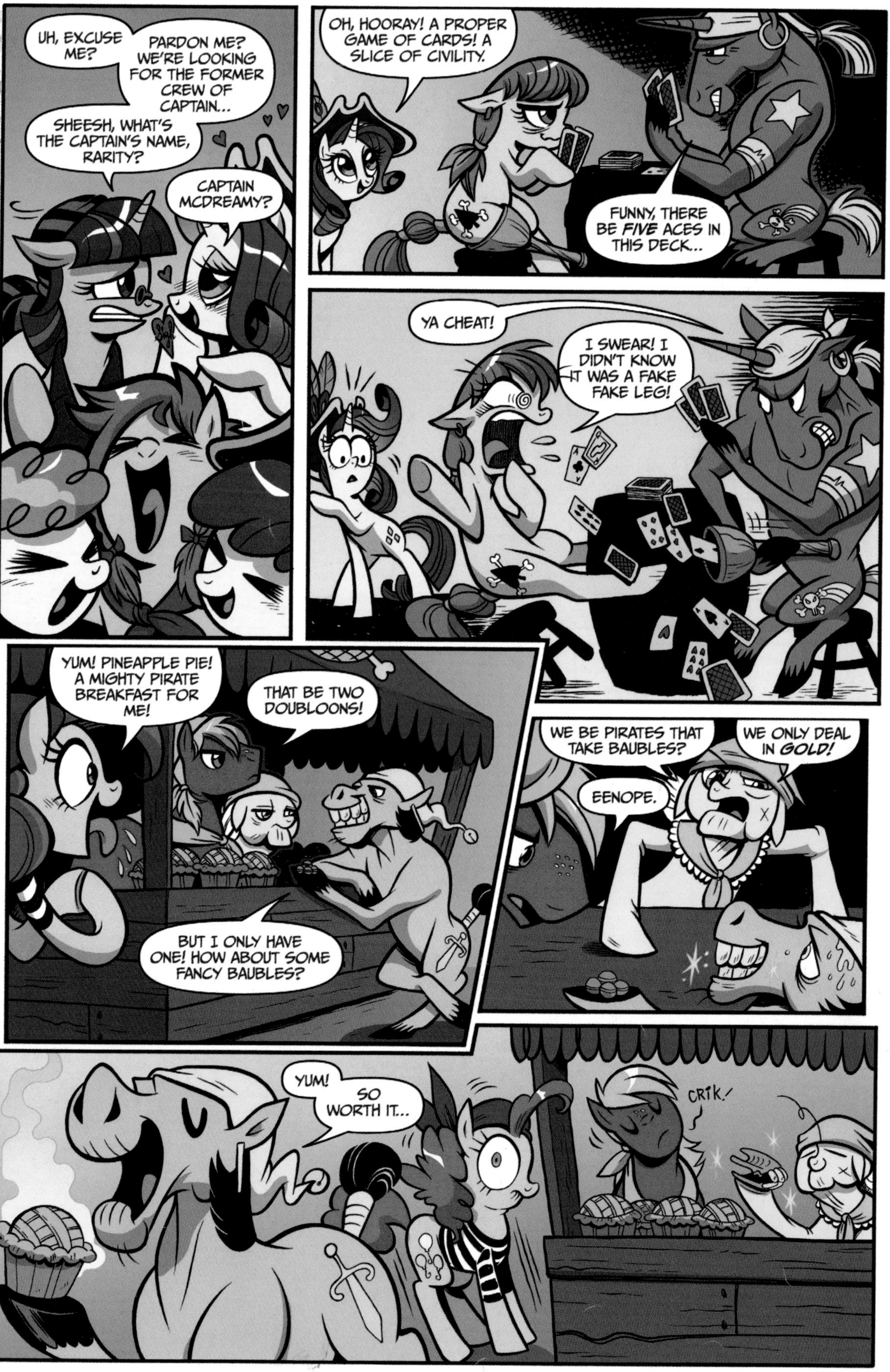
UH, EXCUSE ME?
PARDON ME? WE'RE LOOKING FOR THE FORMER CREW OF CAPTAIN...
SHEESH, WHAT'S THE CAPTAIN'S NAME, RARITY?
CAPTAIN MCDREAMY?
OH, HOORAY! A PROPER GAME OF CARDS! A SLICE OF CIVILITY.
FUNNY, THERE BE FIVE ACES IN THIS DECK...
YA CHEAT!
I SWEAR! I DIDN'T KNOW IT WAS A FAKE FAKE LEG!
YUM! PINEAPPLE PIE! A MIGHTY PIRATE BREAKFAST FOR ME!
THAT BE TWO DOUBLOONS!
BUT I ONLY HAVE ONE! HOW ABOUT SOME FANCY BAUBLES?
WE BE PIRATES THAT TAKE BAUBLES?
EENOPE.
WE ONLY DEAL IN GOLD!
YUM!
SO WORTH IT...
CRIK!

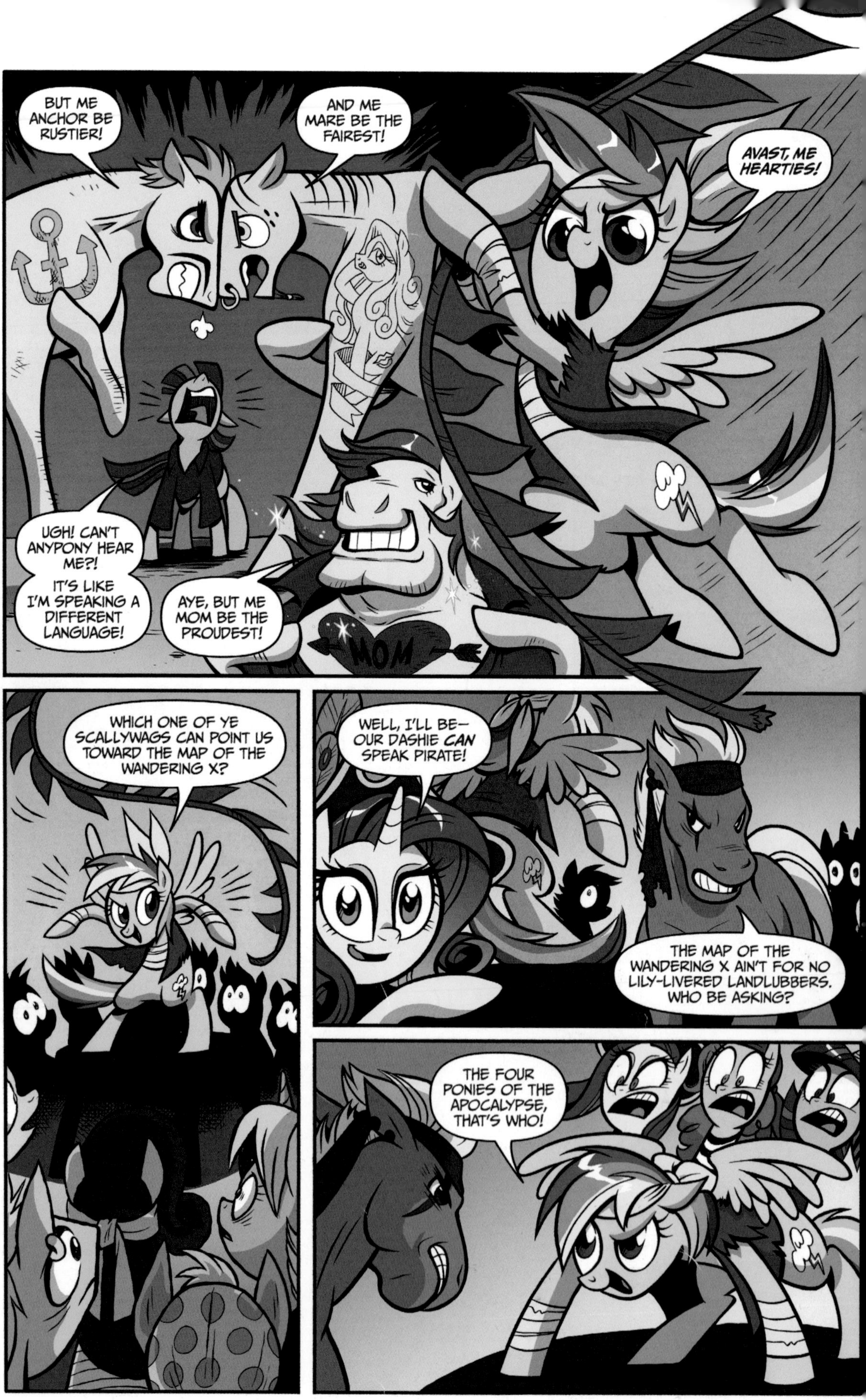
BUT ME ANCHOR BE RUSTIER!
AND ME MARE BE THE FAIREST!
AVAST, ME HEARTIES!
UGH! CAN'T ANYPONY HEAR ME?!
IT'S LIKE I'M SPEAKING A DIFFERENT LANGUAGE!
AYE, BUT ME MOM BE THE PROUDEST!
MOM
WHICH ONE OF YE SCALLYWAGS CAN POINT US TOWARD THE MAP OF THE WANDERING X?
WELL, I'LL BE— OUR DASHIE CAN SPEAK PIRATE!
THE MAP OF THE WANDERING X AIN'T FOR NO LILY-LIVERED LANDLUBBERS. WHO BE ASKING?
THE FOUR PONIES OF THE APOCALYPSE, THAT'S WHO!

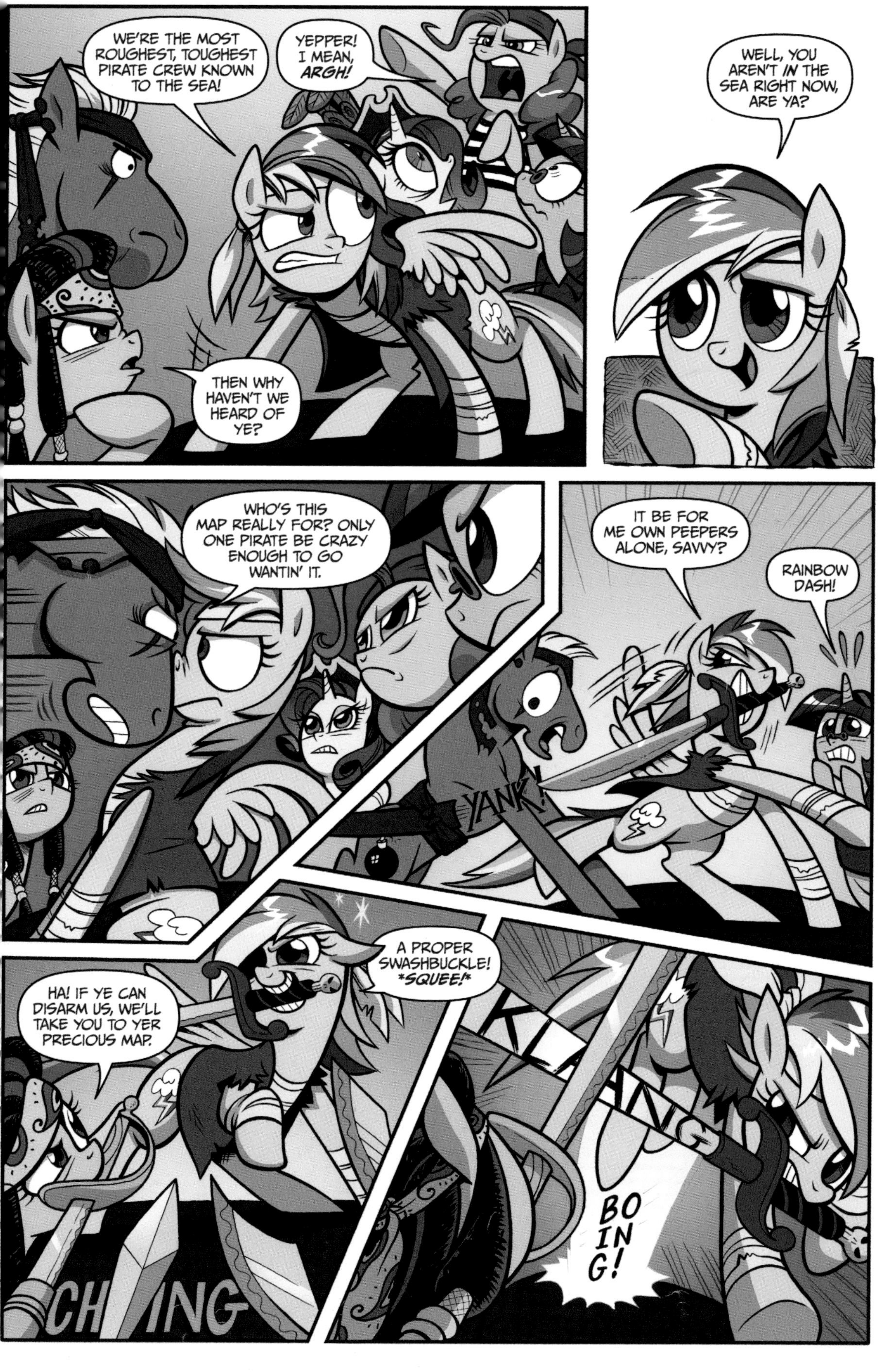

WE'RE THE MOST ROUGHEST, TOUGHEST PIRATE CREW KNOWN TO THE SEA!
YEPPER! I MEAN, ARGH!
THEN WHY HAVEN'T WE HEARD OF YE?
WELL, YOU AREN'T IN THE SEA RIGHT NOW, ARE YA?
WHO'S THIS MAP REALLY FOR? ONLY ONE PIRATE BE CRAZY ENOUGH TO GO WANTIN' IT.
IT BE FOR ME OWN PEEPERS ALONE, SAVVY?
RAINBOW DASH!
YANK!
HA! IF YE CAN DISARM US, WE'LL TAKE YOU TO YER PRECIOUS MAP.
A PROPER SWASHBUCKLE! *SQUEE!*
CH ING
KLANG
BOING!

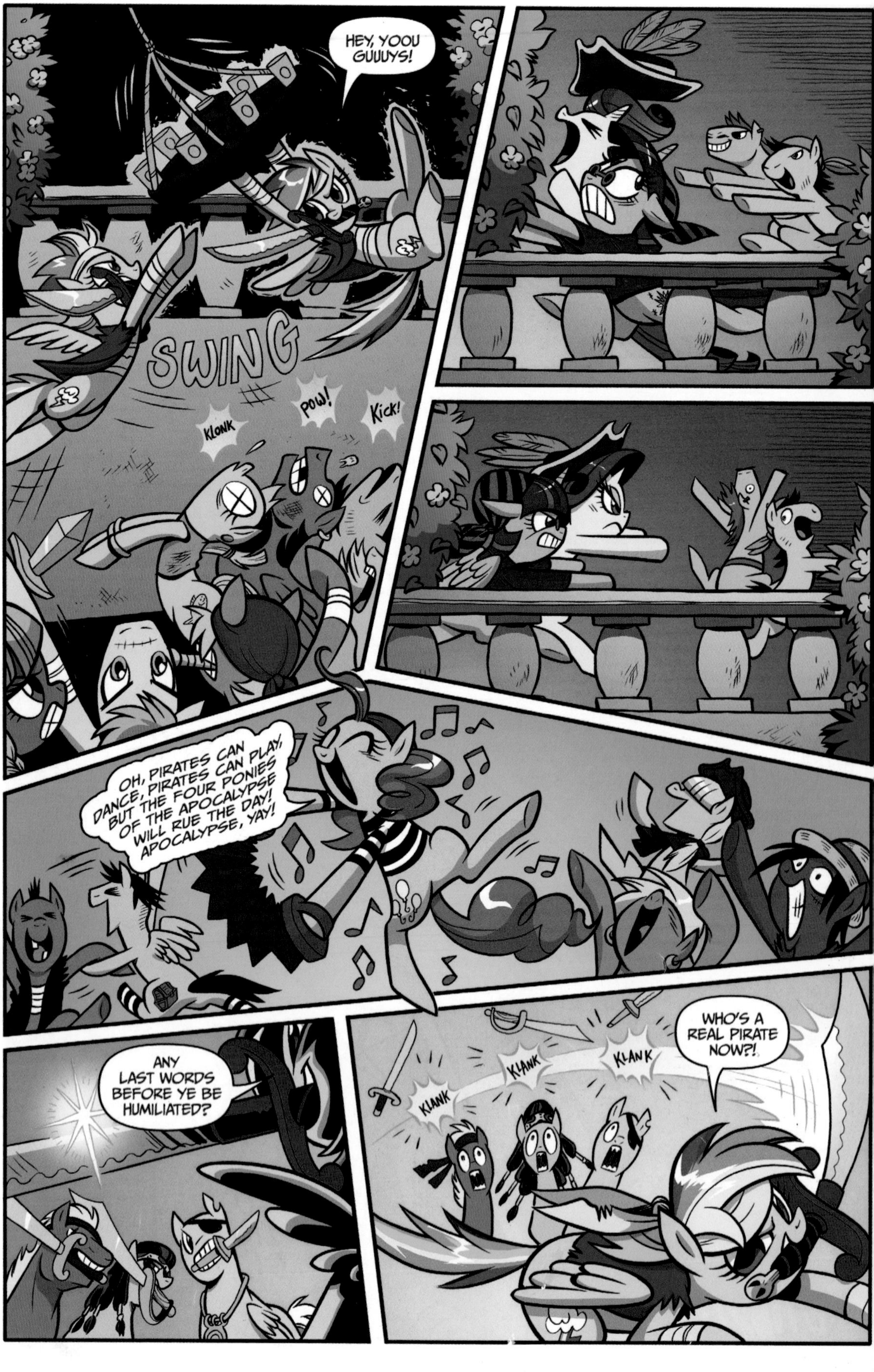
HEY, YOOU GUUUYS!
SWING
KLONK
POW!
KICK!
OH, PIRATES CAN DANCE, PIRATES CAN PLAY, BUT THE FOUR PONIES OF THE APOCALYPSE WILL RUE THE DAY! APOCALYPSE, YAY!
ANY LAST WORDS BEFORE YE BE HUMILIATED?
KLANK
KLANK
KLANK
WHO'S A REAL PIRATE NOW?!

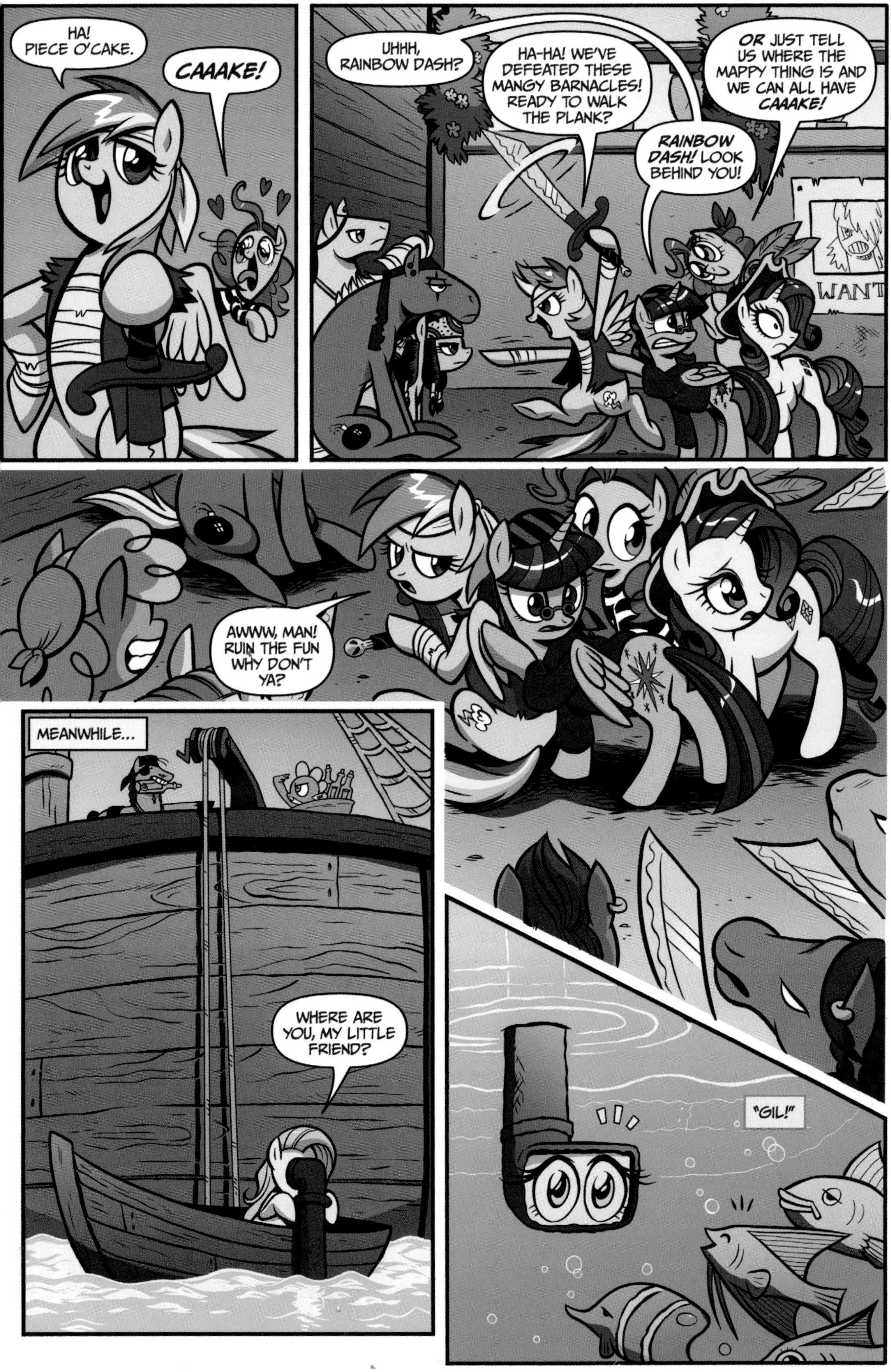
HA!
PIECE O'CAKE.
CAAAKE!
UHHH, RAINBOW DASH?
HA-HA! WE'VE DEFEATED THESE MANGY BARNACLES! READY TO WALK THE PLANK?
RAINBOW DASH! LOOK BEHIND YOU!
OR JUST TELL US WHERE THE MAPPY THING IS AND WE CAN ALL HAVE CAAAKE!
WANT
AWWW, MAN! RUIN THE FUN WHY DON'T YA?
MEANWHILE...
WHERE ARE YOU, MY LITTLE FRIEND?
"GIL!"

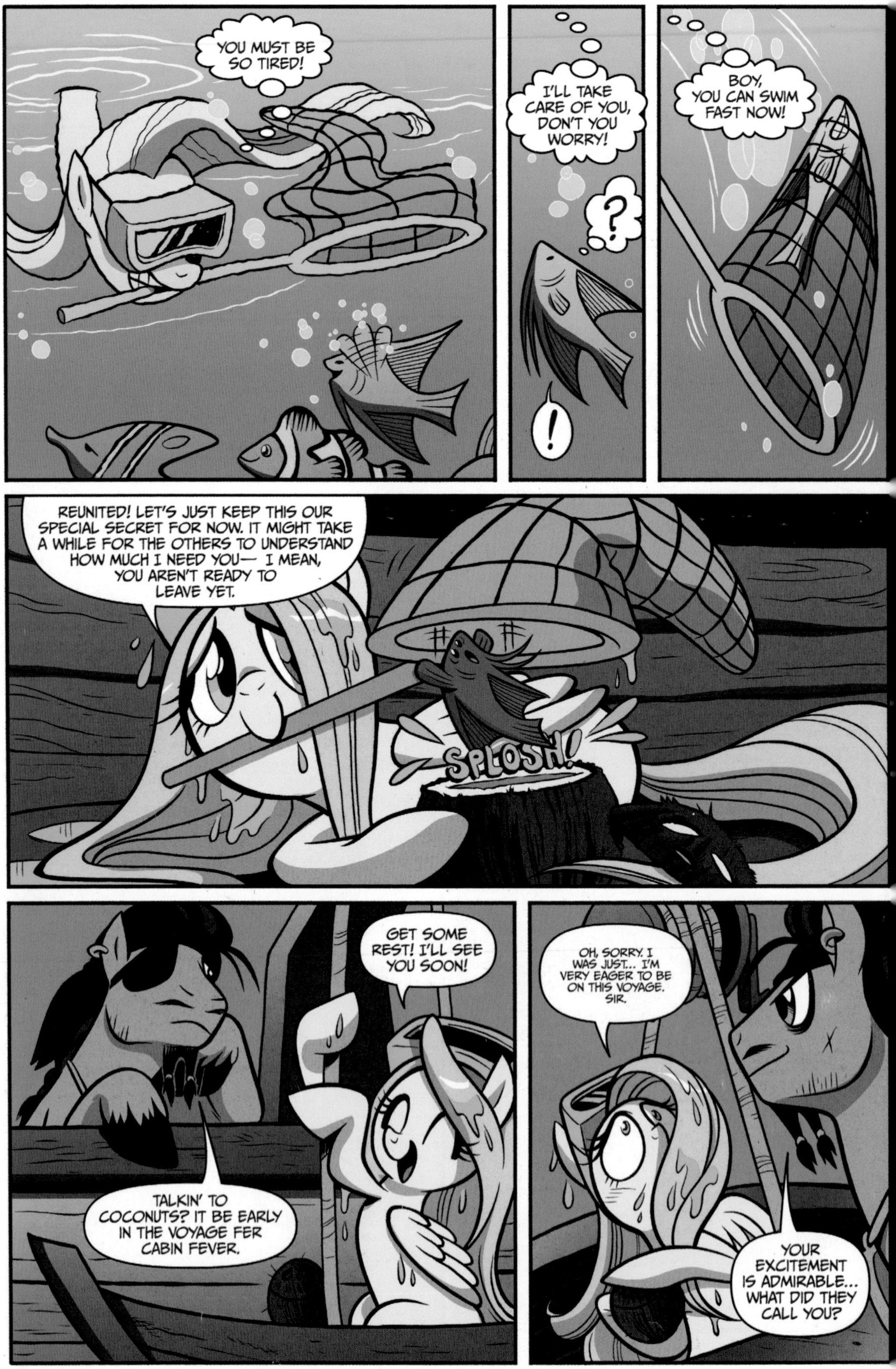
YOU MUST BE SO TIRED!
I'LL TAKE CARE OF YOU, DON'T YOU WORRY!
?
!
BOY, YOU CAN SWIM FAST NOW!
REUNITED! LET'S JUST KEEP THIS OUR SPECIAL SECRET FOR NOW. IT MIGHT TAKE A WHILE FOR THE OTHERS TO UNDERSTAND HOW MUCH I NEED YOU— I MEAN, YOU AREN'T READY TO LEAVE YET.
SPLOSH!
GET SOME REST! I'LL SEE YOU SOON!
TALKIN' TO COCONUTS? IT BE EARLY IN THE VOYAGE FER CABIN FEVER.
OH, SORRY. I WAS JUST... I'M VERY EAGER TO BE ON THIS VOYAGE. SIR.
YOUR EXCITEMENT IS ADMIRABLE... WHAT DID THEY CALL YOU?

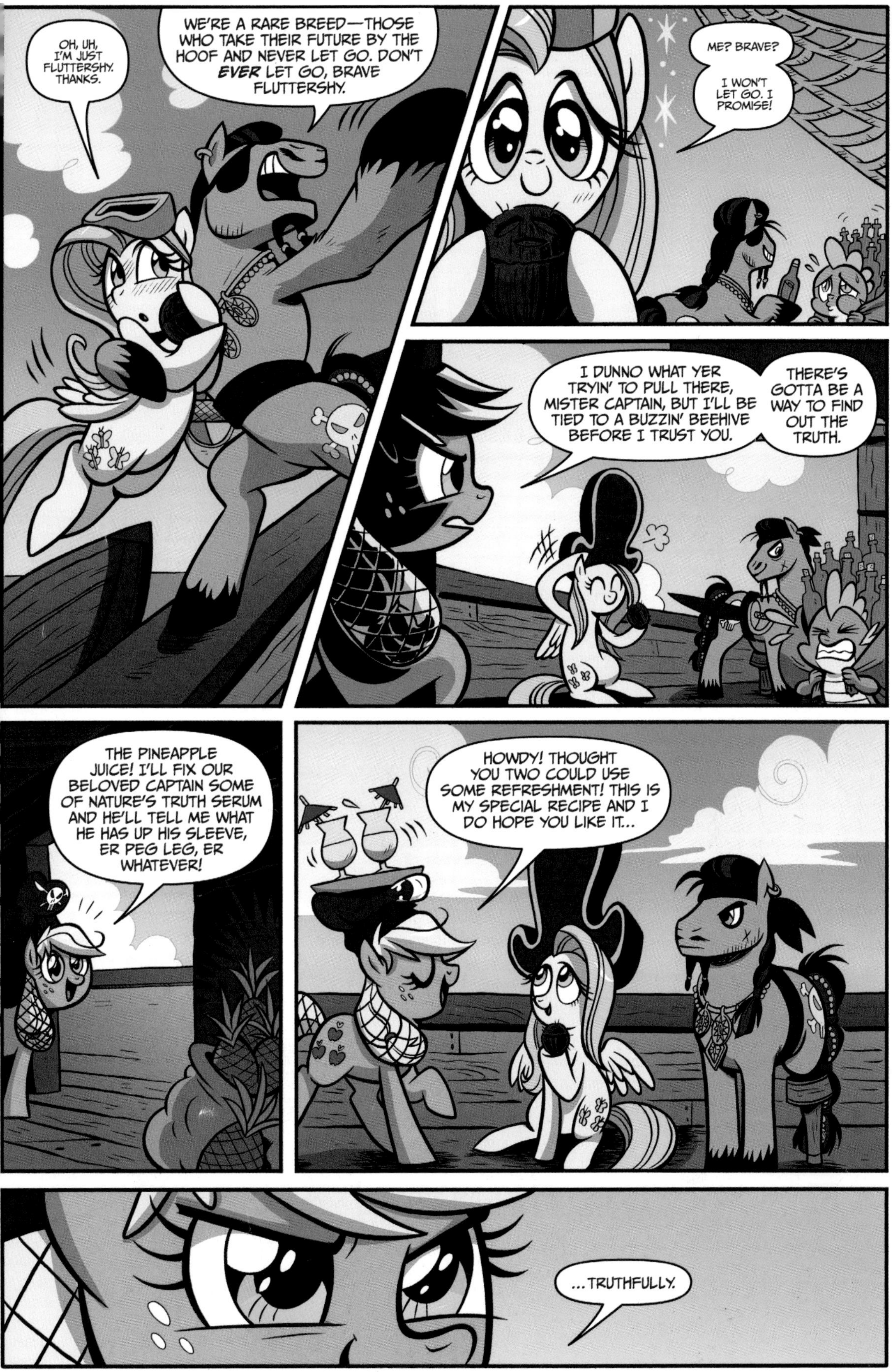
OH, UH, I'M JUST FLUTTERSHY. THANKS.
WE'RE A RARE BREED—THOSE WHO TAKE THEIR FUTURE BY THE HOOF AND NEVER LET GO. DON'T **EVER** LET GO, BRAVE FLUTTERSHY.
ME? BRAVE?
I WON'T LET GO. I PROMISE!
I DUNNO WHAT YER TRYIN' TO PULL THERE, MISTER CAPTAIN, BUT I'LL BE TIED TO A BUZZIN' BEEHIVE BEFORE I TRUST YOU.
THERE'S GOTTA BE A WAY TO FIND OUT THE TRUTH.
THE PINEAPPLE JUICE! I'LL FIX OUR BELOVED CAPTAIN SOME OF NATURE'S TRUTH SERUM AND HE'LL TELL ME WHAT HE HAS UP HIS SLEEVE, ER PEG LEG, ER WHATEVER!
HOWDY! THOUGHT YOU TWO COULD USE SOME REFRESHMENT! THIS IS MY SPECIAL RECIPE AND I DO HOPE YOU LIKE IT...
...TRUTHFULLY.

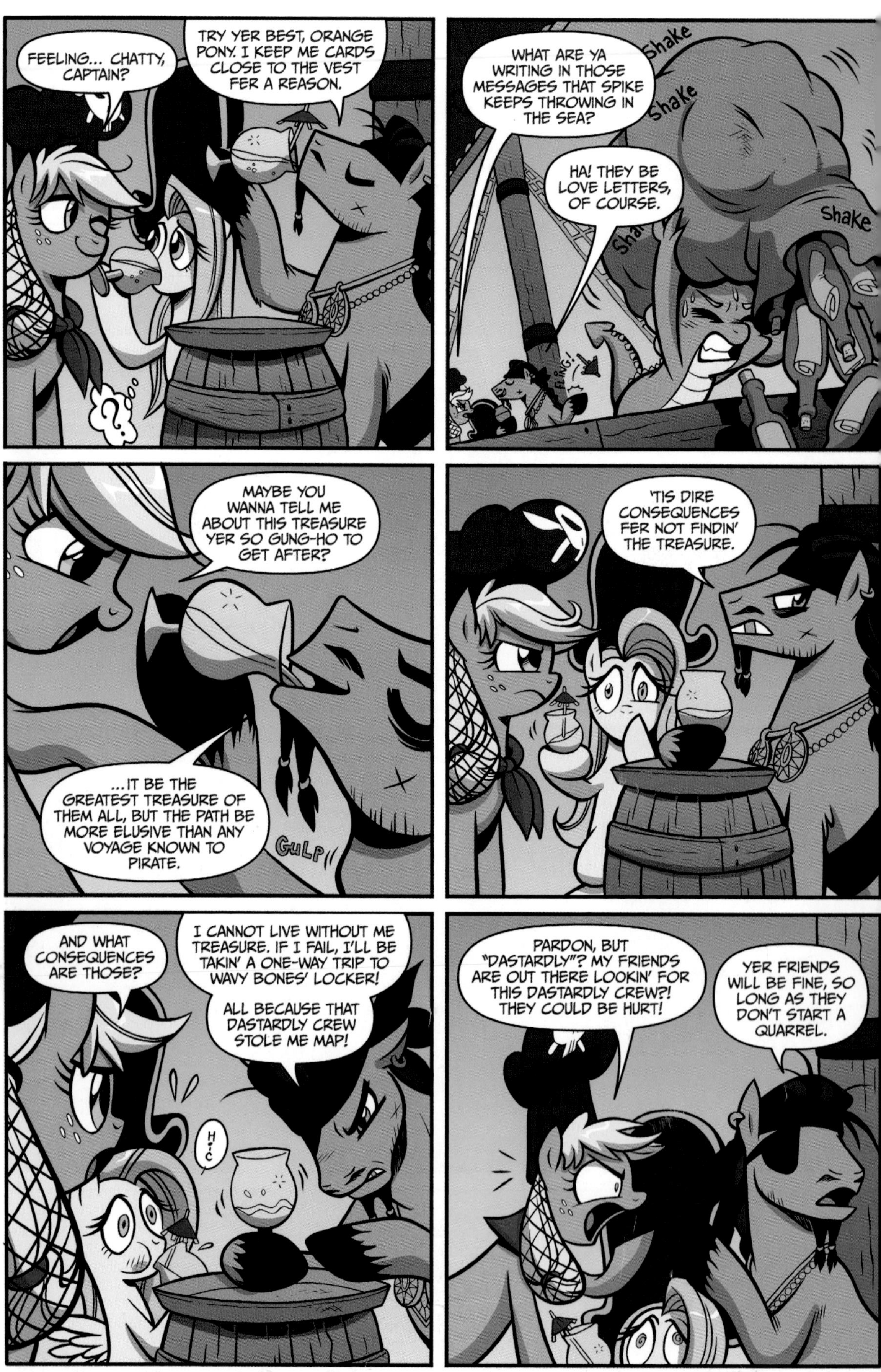
FEELING… CHATTY, CAPTAIN?
TRY YER BEST, ORANGE PONY. I KEEP ME CARDS CLOSE TO THE VEST FER A REASON.
WHAT ARE YA WRITING IN THOSE MESSAGES THAT SPIKE KEEPS THROWING IN THE SEA?
Shake Shake Shake
HA! THEY BE LOVE LETTERS, OF COURSE.
MAYBE YOU WANNA TELL ME ABOUT THIS TREASURE YER SO GUNG-HO TO GET AFTER?
…IT BE THE GREATEST TREASURE OF THEM ALL, BUT THE PATH BE MORE ELUSIVE THAN ANY VOYAGE KNOWN TO PIRATE.
GuLP
'TIS DIRE CONSEQUENCES FER NOT FINDIN' THE TREASURE.
AND WHAT CONSEQUENCES ARE THOSE?
I CANNOT LIVE WITHOUT ME TREASURE. IF I FAIL, I'LL BE TAKIN' A ONE-WAY TRIP TO WAVY BONES' LOCKER!
ALL BECAUSE THAT DASTARDLY CREW STOLE ME MAP!
HIC
PARDON, BUT "DASTARDLY"? MY FRIENDS ARE OUT THERE LOOKIN' FOR THIS DASTARDLY CREW?! THEY COULD BE HURT!
YER FRIENDS WILL BE FINE, SO LONG AS THEY DON'T START A QUARREL.

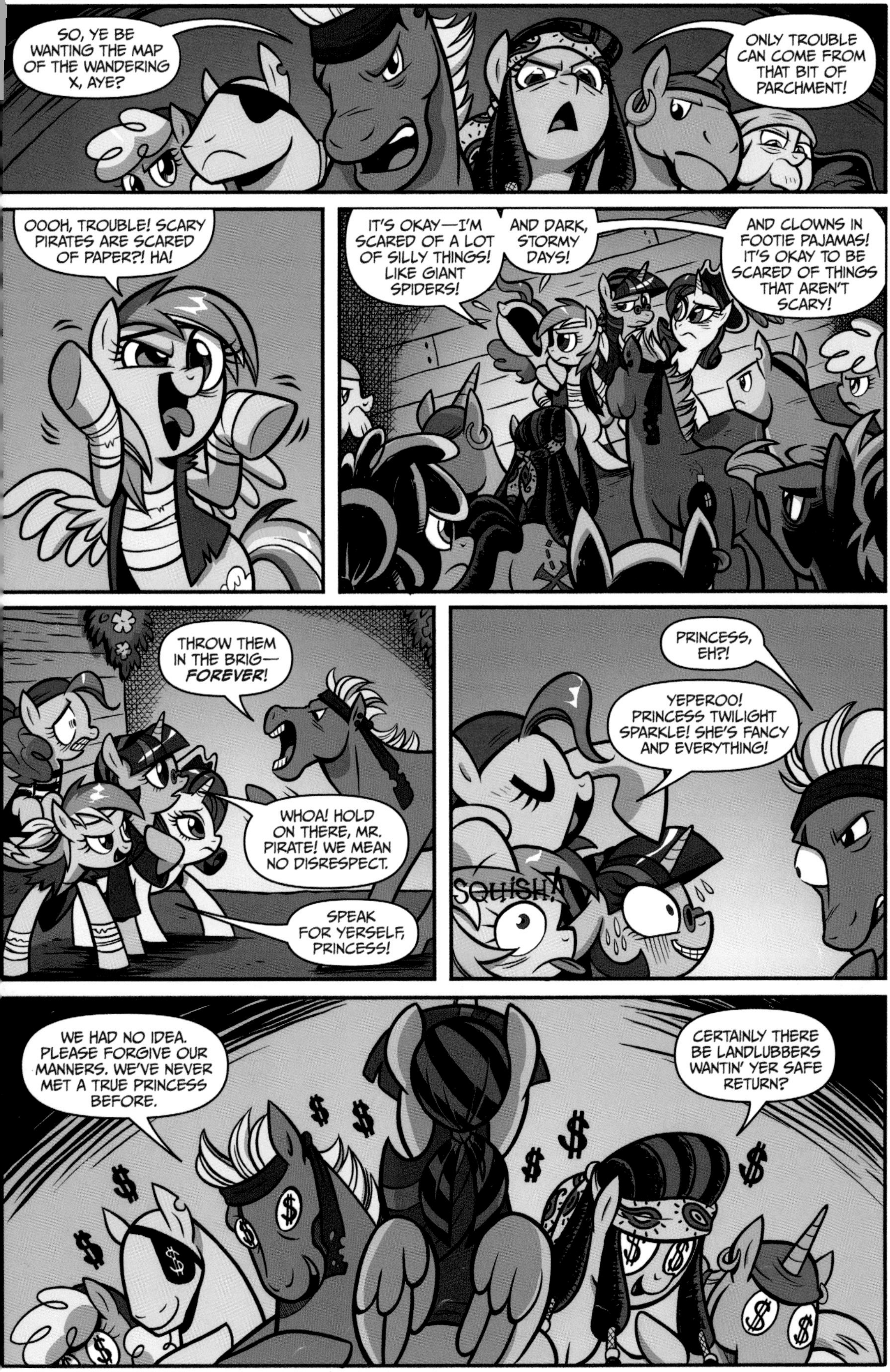
SO, YE BE WANTING THE MAP OF THE WANDERING X, AYE?
ONLY TROUBLE CAN COME FROM THAT BIT OF PARCHMENT!
OOOH, TROUBLE! SCARY PIRATES ARE SCARED OF PAPER?! HA!
IT'S OKAY—I'M SCARED OF A LOT OF SILLY THINGS! LIKE GIANT SPIDERS!
AND DARK, STORMY DAYS!
AND CLOWNS IN FOOTIE PAJAMAS! IT'S OKAY TO BE SCARED OF THINGS THAT AREN'T SCARY!
THROW THEM IN THE BRIG— *FOREVER*!
WHOA! HOLD ON THERE, MR. PIRATE! WE MEAN NO DISRESPECT.
SPEAK FOR YERSELF, PRINCESS!
PRINCESS, EH?!
YEPEROO! PRINCESS TWILIGHT SPARKLE! SHE'S FANCY AND EVERYTHING!
SQUISH!
WE HAD NO IDEA. PLEASE FORGIVE OUR MANNERS. WE'VE NEVER MET A TRUE PRINCESS BEFORE.
CERTAINLY THERE BE LANDLUBBERS WANTIN' YER SAFE RETURN?

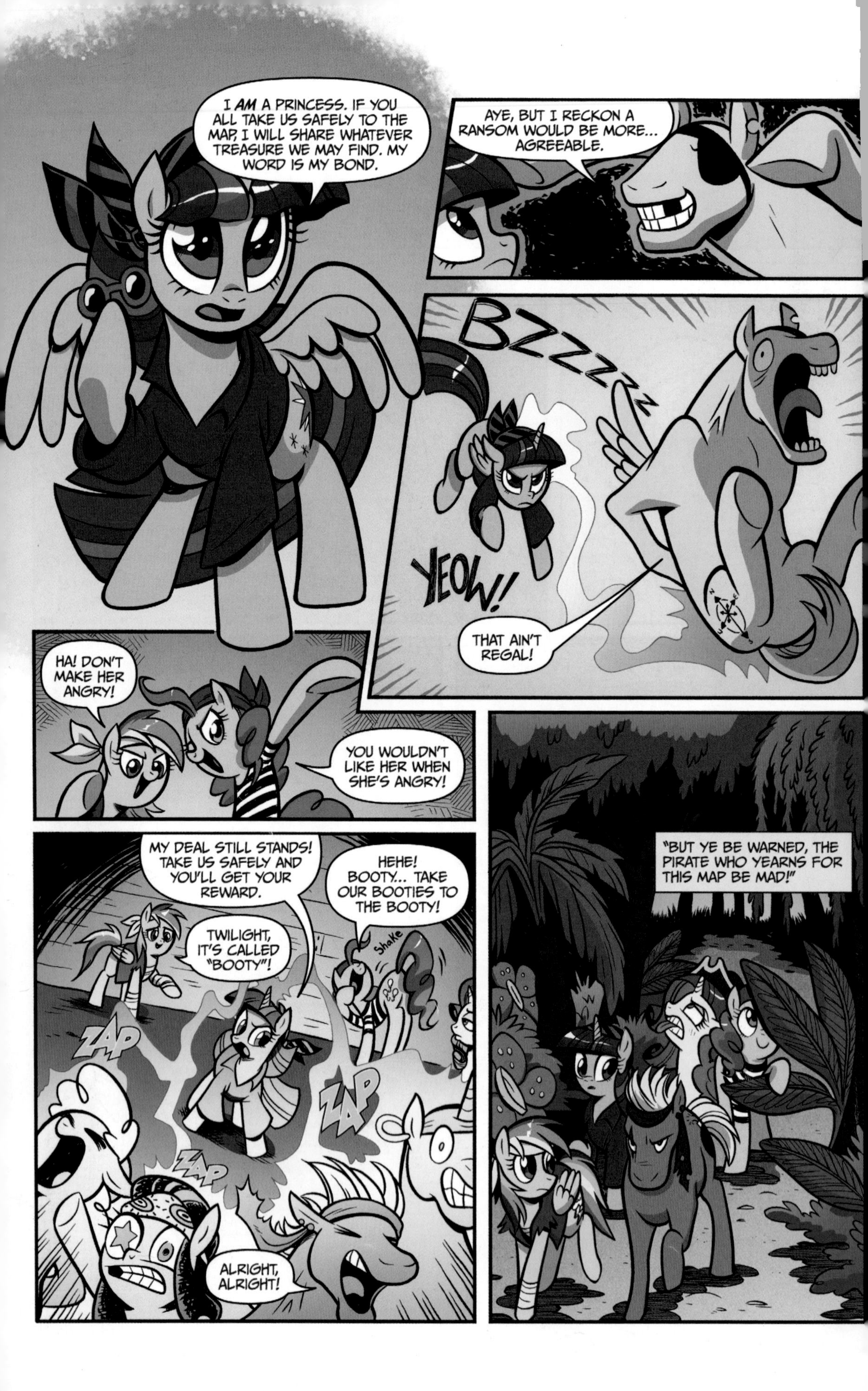
I *AM* A PRINCESS. IF YOU ALL TAKE US SAFELY TO THE MAP, I WILL SHARE WHATEVER TREASURE WE MAY FIND. MY WORD IS MY BOND.
AYE, BUT I RECKON A RANSOM WOULD BE MORE... AGREEABLE.
BZZZZZZ
YEOW!
THAT AIN'T REGAL!
HA! DON'T MAKE HER ANGRY!
YOU WOULDN'T LIKE HER WHEN SHE'S ANGRY!
MY DEAL STILL STANDS! TAKE US SAFELY AND YOU'LL GET YOUR REWARD.
TWILIGHT, IT'S CALLED "BOOTY"!
HEHE! BOOTY... TAKE OUR BOOTIES TO THE BOOTY!
Shake
ZAP
ZAP
ZAP
ALRIGHT, ALRIGHT!
"BUT YE BE WARNED, THE PIRATE WHO YEARNS FOR THIS MAP BE MAD!"

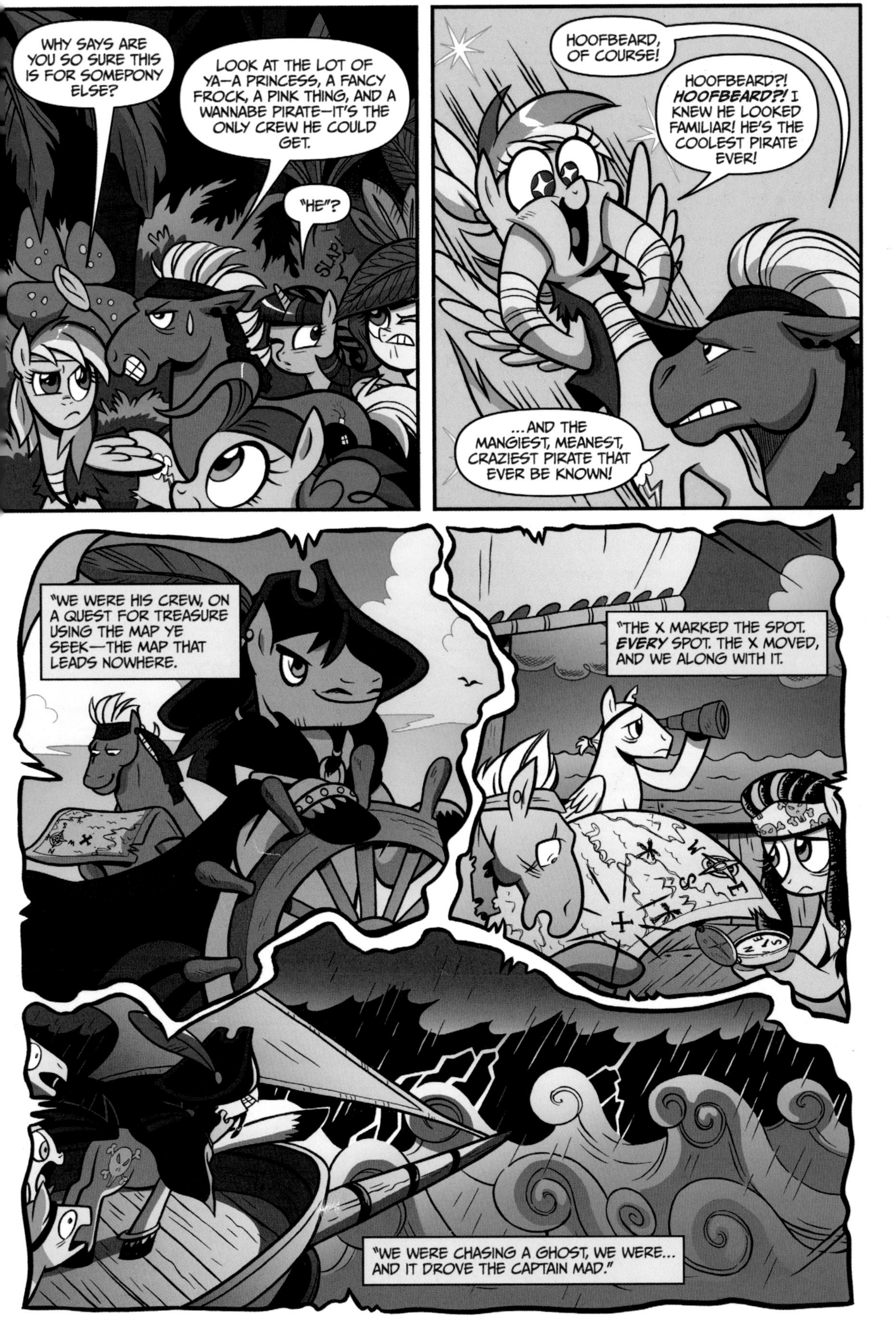
WHY SAYS ARE YOU SO SURE THIS IS FOR SOMEPONY ELSE?
LOOK AT THE LOT OF YA—A PRINCESS, A FANCY FROCK, A PINK THING, AND A WANNABE PIRATE—IT'S THE ONLY CREW HE COULD GET.
"HE"?
SLAP!
HOOFBEARD, OF COURSE!
HOOFBEARD?! HOOFBEARD?! I KNEW HE LOOKED FAMILIAR! HE'S THE COOLEST PIRATE EVER!
...AND THE MANGIEST, MEANEST, CRAZIEST PIRATE THAT EVER BE KNOWN!
"WE WERE HIS CREW, ON A QUEST FOR TREASURE USING THE MAP YE SEEK—THE MAP THAT LEADS NOWHERE.
"THE X MARKED THE SPOT. EVERY SPOT. THE X MOVED, AND WE ALONG WITH IT.
"WE WERE CHASING A GHOST, WE WERE... AND IT DROVE THE CAPTAIN MAD."

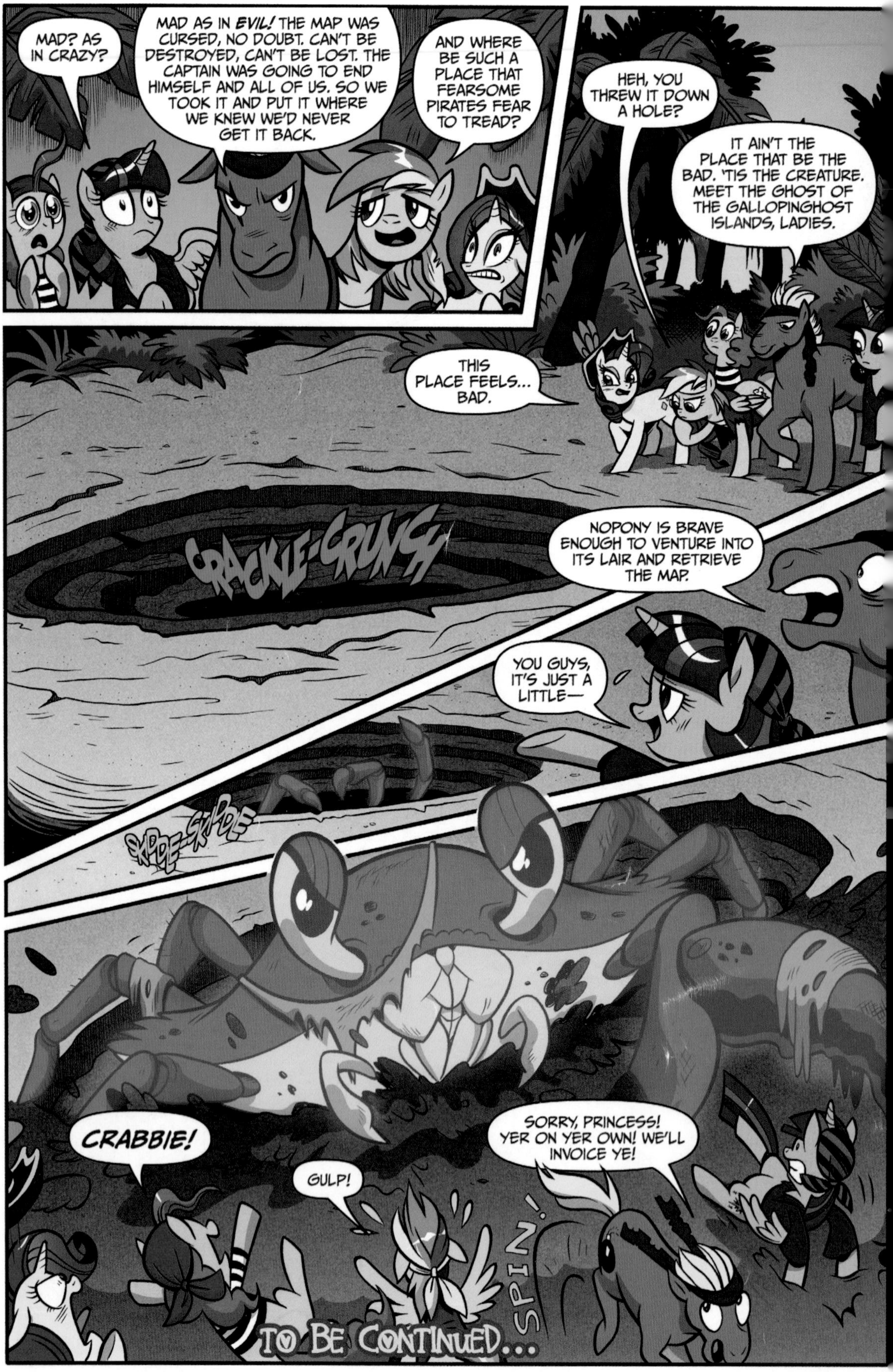

MAD? AS IN CRAZY?
MAD AS IN *EVIL!* THE MAP WAS CURSED, NO DOUBT. CAN'T BE DESTROYED, CAN'T BE LOST. THE CAPTAIN WAS GOING TO END HIMSELF AND ALL OF US. SO WE TOOK IT AND PUT IT WHERE WE KNEW WE'D NEVER GET IT BACK.
AND WHERE BE SUCH A PLACE THAT FEARSOME PIRATES FEAR TO TREAD?
HEH, YOU THREW IT DOWN A HOLE?
IT AIN'T THE PLACE THAT BE THE BAD. 'TIS THE CREATURE. MEET THE GHOST OF THE GALLOPINGHOST ISLANDS, LADIES.
THIS PLACE FEELS... BAD.
CRACKLE-CRUNCH
NOPONY IS BRAVE ENOUGH TO VENTURE INTO ITS LAIR AND RETRIEVE THE MAP.
YOU GUYS, IT'S JUST A LITTLE—
SKIDDLE-SKIDDLE
CRABBIE!
GULP!
SORRY, PRINCESS! YER ON YER OWN! WE'LL INVOICE YE!
SPIN!
TO BE CONTINUED...